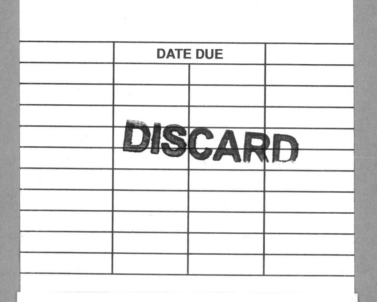

ROTTEN RALPH'S
ROTTEN
CHRISTMAS

Written by Jack Gantos
Illustrated by Nicole Rubel

Houghton Mifflin Company Boston

To Kaelin

— J.G.

To my family

— N.R.

Library of Congress Cataloging in Publication Data

Gantos, Jack.
    Rotten Ralph's rotten Christmas.

    Summary: Rotten Ralph, the cat, is not at all nice to
the Christmas visitor.
    [1. Cats — Fiction. 2. Behavior — Fiction. 3. Christmas
— Fiction] I. Rubel, Nicole, ill. II. Title.
PZ7.G15334Rok   1984   [E]   84-664
ISBN 0-395-35380-7

Printed in the United States of America

**RNF ISBN 0-395-35380-7
PAP ISBN 0-395-45685-1**

WOZ   20 19 18 17 16 15 14 13 12 11

Rotten Ralph is Sarah's cat.

Rotten Ralph loved to be rotten.

When Sarah knitted Ralph a sweater,

he unraveled all her work.

"You shouldn't be so rotten,"

said Sarah.

When Sarah practiced her Christmas carols,
Rotten Ralph walked across the piano keys.

"Sometimes you're very difficult
to love, Ralph," said Sarah.

Ralph just stuck out his tongue
and went to bed.

The next morning when Rotten Ralph woke up, a very sweet cat was sitting on Sarah's lap.

"This is Percy," said Sarah. "He's our new friend and I want you to make him feel at home."

Rotten Ralph tried to be nice.

He showed Percy how to throw snowballs.

"Good cats don't throw snowballs,"
said Sarah. "Now come inside and help
Percy and me put up the Christmas
decorations."

When Percy hung up his Christmas stocking,
Rotten Ralph cut a hole in it.

"You better behave yourself," said Sarah.
"Bad cats don't get Christmas presents."

When Percy put together the train set,
Rotten Ralph tied him across the tracks.
"You're not being very helpful,"
said Sarah.

When Percy went to hang the
star on the Christmas tree
Rotten Ralph pulled the ladder from
under his feet.

"You are a bad cat," Sarah said to
Ralph. "You should be more like Percy."

"I'm not a goody-goody,"
Ralph said to himself.

He ate the milk and cookies
Percy had left out for Santa Claus.

Percy was upset.

"That's not a very nice thing
to do," said Sarah.

That night Sarah decided to read
Percy and Ralph a Christmas story.

But when Rotten Ralph went to sit
on Sarah's lap, Percy was already there.

Instead of listening to the story,
Ralph banged on his toy drum.

"Stop that," said Sarah.

"I've had enough of this,"
Rotten Ralph said. "Percy's
getting everything."

He sneaked under the Christmas tree
and put "Ralph" on all
of Percy's gifts.

Later, when Rotten Ralph went to
bed, he found that Percy had already
taken his place.

"Sarah loves him more than she
loves me," Ralph said to himself.

On Christmas morning Rotten Ralph ripped open all the presents. But he didn't like any of them. There was a big floppy bow, a cute, pink teddy bear, and a pair of fuzzy slippers.

"These gifts belong to Percy," said Sarah.

Just then there was a knock at the door.

Sarah smiled. "This must be Percy's owner coming to take him home," she said.

"I thought he was going to stay forever," Rotten Ralph said to himself.

After Percy left there were no
more presents left under the tree.

Rotten Ralph felt rotten.

Then Sarah said, "Now it's time
for us to exchange gifts."

She gave Ralph a new red bicycle.
Rotten Ralph gave Sarah a picture
of himself.

Then he jumped onto Sarah's lap.

"You weren't jealous of that other

cat, were you?" she asked.

"Not me," Ralph said to himself.

"Nobody can take my place."